# RACE AROUND THE WORLD!

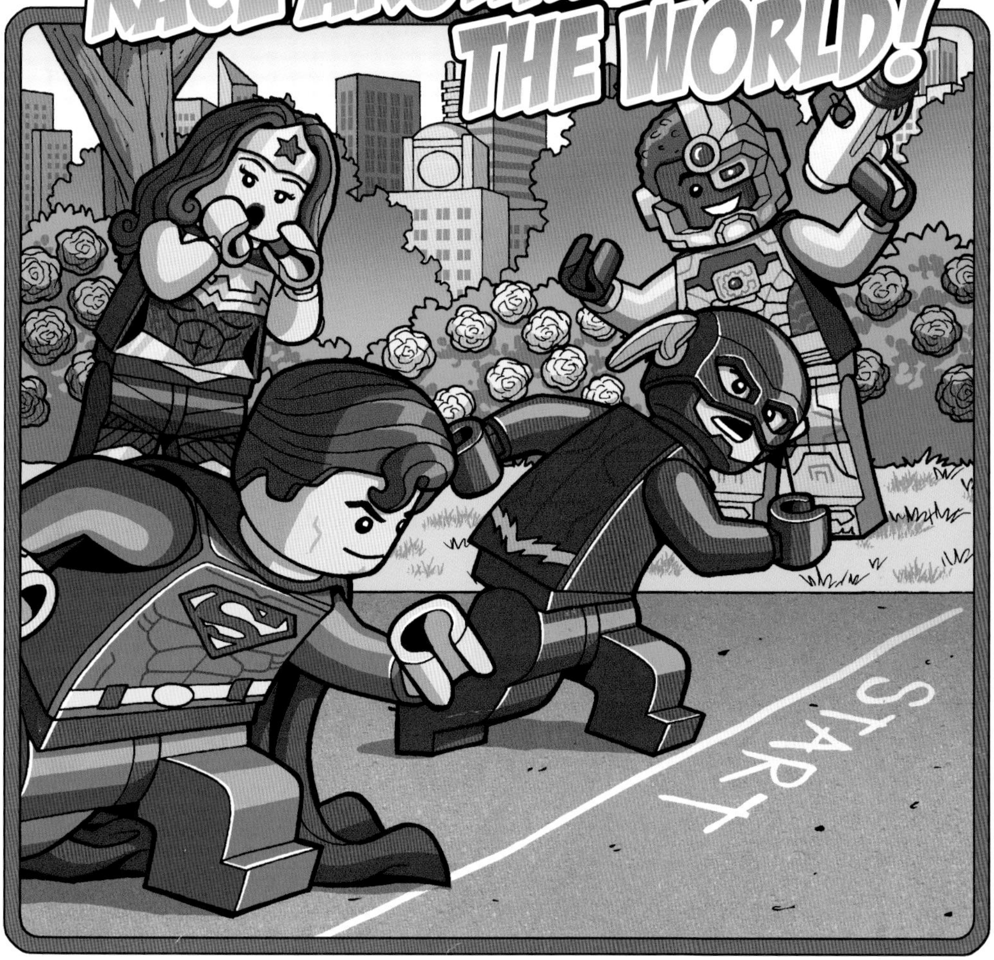

BY TREY KING  ILLUSTRATED BY SEAN WANG

SCHOLASTIC CHILDREN'S BOOKS
EUSTON HOUSE,
24 EVERSHOLT STREET,
LONDON NW1 1DB, UK

A DIVISION OF SCHOLASTIC LTD
LONDON ~ NEW YORK ~ TORONTO ~ SYDNEY ~ AUCKLAND
MEXICO CITY ~ NEW DELHI ~ HONG KONG

THIS BOOK WAS FIRST PUBLISHED IN THE US IN 2016 BY SCHOLASTIC INC.
PUBLISHED IN THE UK BY SCHOLASTIC LTD, 2016

ISBN 978 1407 16221 8

PRINTED AND BOUND IN ITALY

2 4 6 8 10 9 7 5 3 1

WONDER WOMAN TELLS HER FRIENDS THAT IT DOESN'T MATTER WHO IS FASTER. BUT SUPERMAN AND THE FLASH WANT TO KNOW.

THESE HEROES ARE SO FAST, THEY'RE ALREADY HALFWAY ACROSS THE OCEAN! BUT SUPERMAN HAS SUPER-HEARING, AND HE HEARS SOMEONE WHO NEEDS HELP.

SUPERMAN DIVES DEEP INTO THE OCEAN. AQUAMAN IS BATTLING HIS ENEMY BLACK MANTA! WATCH OUT FOR THOSE SHARKS!

"I GUESS SUPERMAN REALIZED HE CAN'T BEAT ME," THE FLASH SAYS. "I KNEW THAT HE COULDN'T OUTRUN ME!"

BUT THE FLASH SPOKE TOO SOON . . .

"THANKS FOR THE SAVE, FLASH," HAWKMAN SAYS.

"NO PROBLEM," THE FLASH SAYS, RETURNING TO THE RACE. "BUT WATCH OUT. I THINK GRODD IS ABOUT TO LOSE HIS BANANAS."

MEANWHILE, SUPERMAN IS FAR AHEAD NOW, RACING THROUGH THE SNOWY MOUNTAINS. BUT USING HIS SUPER-VISION, HE SEES THAT ANOTHER ONE OF HIS FRIENDS NEEDS HELP . . .

ELSEWHERE, GREEN LANTERN IS IN TROUBLE. SINESTRO KNOCKED HIM OUT OF THE SKY AND IS ABOUT TO SMASH HIM WITH A HAMMER . . .

WHO WON? SUPERMAN? THE FLASH? WONDER WOMAN TOOK A PICTURE TO SEE WHO THE WINNER IS.